D1540741

My Day

Written and illustrated by Heidi Goennel

Seasons
When I Grow Up…
My Day

Illustrated by Heidi Goennel

in Just- spring

My Day

Heidi Goennel

Little, Brown and Company

Boston · Toronto

3 1172 06604 1435

Copyright © 1988 by Heidi Goennel

All rights reserved. No part of this book may be
reproduced in any form or by any electronic or
mechanical means, including information storage
and retrieval systems, without permission in
writing from the publisher, except by a reviewer
who may quote brief passages in a review.

First Edition

Library of Congress Cataloging-in-Publication Data

Goennel, Heidi.
My Day.

Summary: Follows a child from morning to bedtime,
experiencing such events of the day as having breakfast,
going to school, and playing hide-and-go-seek.
I. Title.
PZ7.G554My   1988   [E]   87-37858
ISBN 0-316-31839-6

10 9 8 7 6 5 4 3 2 1

NIL

Published simultaneously in Canada
by Little, Brown & Company (Canada) Limited

Printed in Italy

To A.S.G.

I love to get up every morning
and start a brand-new day.
My day begins when…

I wake up early

and get dressed

and eat a big breakfast.

Then I take the bus to school.

I do a lot of reading and writing

and also take violin lessons.

Soon it's time for lunch.

Then I have art class —

it's my favorite!

After school I go home

and play with my friends.

Sometimes I go for a bike ride alone

or play hide-and-go-seek.

Just before dinner I do my chores.

Later on I watch television

or read a good story.

But I also have to do my school work.

After my bath I write in my diary about my day.

Then I go to sleep

and dream about tomorrow.